For Flinn – GA

For Cherry and Tony – VC

ORCHARD BOOKS
96 Leonard Street, London EC2A 4XD
Orchard Books Australia
14 Mars Road, Lane Cove, NSW 2066
ISBN 1 86039 791 3 (hardback)
ISBN 1 84121 395 0 (paperback)
First published in Great Britain in 1999
Text © Purple Enterprises Ltd 1999
Illustrations © Vanessa Cabban 1999
The rights of Giles Andreae to be identified as the author and
Vanessa Cabban as illustrator of this book have been asserted by them
in accordance with the Copyright, Designs and Patents Act, 1988.
A CIP catalogue record for this book is available from the British Library.
2 3 4 5 6 7 8 9 10 (hardback)
1 2 3 4 5 6 7 8 9 10 (paperback)
Printed in Hong Kong/China

Love is a Handful of Honey

written by
Giles Andreae

illustrated by
Vanessa Cabban

 ORCHARD BOOKS

Love is that full of beans feeling
That makes you leap out of your bed,

Love is what makes you throw open the curtains
And somersault round on your head.

Love is that warm cosy feeling
You get when you cuddle your Mum,

And love is that feeling of laughing out loud
When somebody tickles your tum.

Love's skipping out in the morning
And hoping the day never ends,

And love's what you feel when you all get together
And go on adventures with friends.

Love's when you hide in the forest
In places that nobody knows,

Love is that fluttery feeling you feel
When a butterfly tickles your toes.

Love is a handful of honey,
And love's making friends with the bees,

Even the flowers are bursting with love
When they're dancing about in the breeze.

And then when your tummies are grumbly,
Love is unwrapping your treats,

And love's stuffing everything all in at once
Leaving masses of mess on your cheeks.

Love is splish-splashing through puddles,
And love's getting soaked in the rain . . .

Love is a rainbow that bursts through the sky
When the sun begins shining again.

Love's when you can't stop describing
Just what you've been doing all day,

And love is when somebody quietly listens
To everything you've got to say.

Love is a great bedtime story
That takes you to faraway lands,

And love's when you want to show someone you care
So you snuggle up close and hold hands.

Love's looking out of the window
To wave at the Man in the Moon,

And love's when you whisper goodnight to the stars
Who'll be watching you dream very soon.

And then when you're tired and sleepy,
And you're cosily tucked up all tight,

Love is that last little cuddle and kiss
That helps you sleep safe through the night...

Goodnight

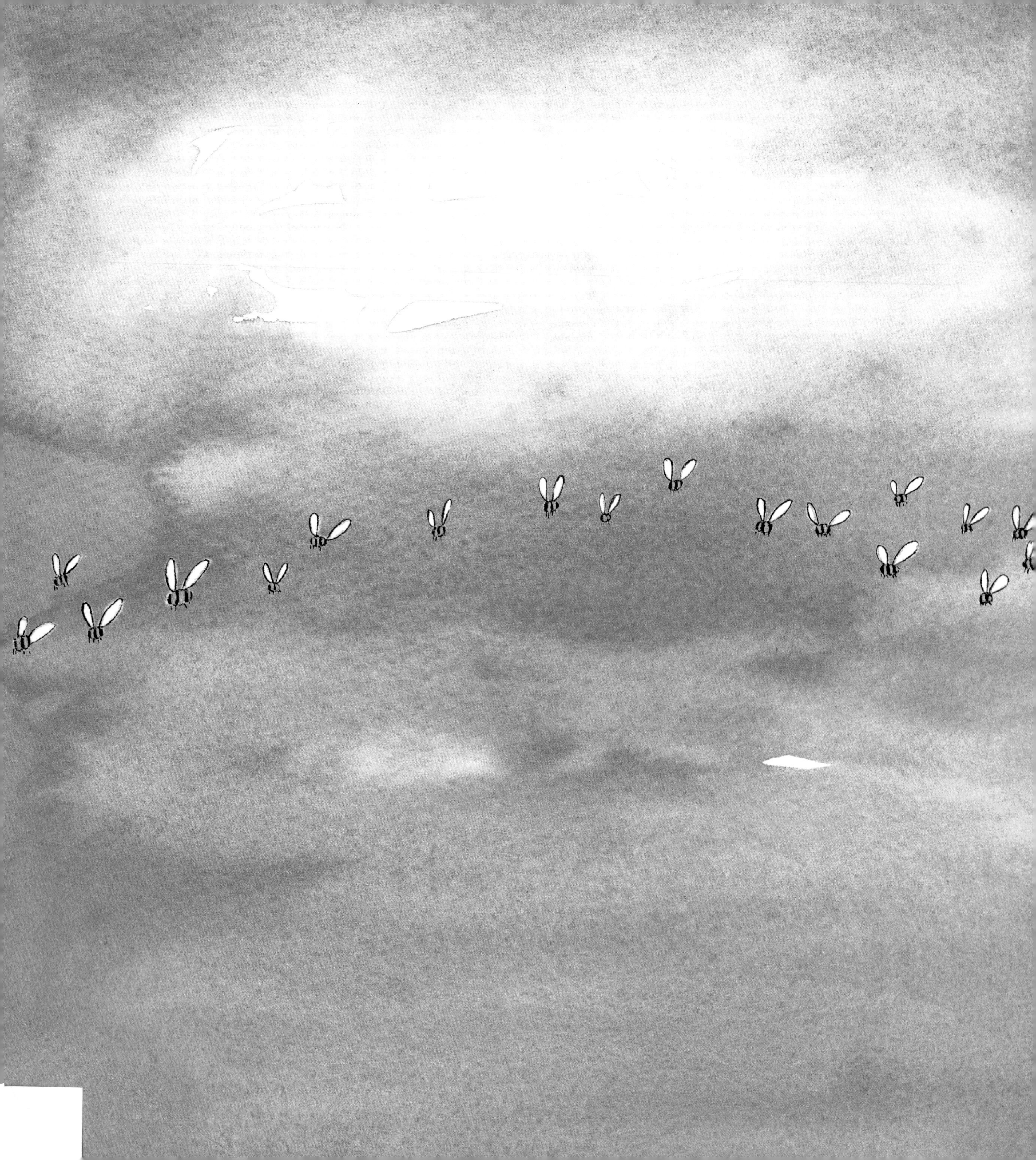